BAD Nana

ALL the FUN OF the FaiR

D1353530

*For Kitty, Tom and Barnaby,
three of the winningest
people I know x x x*

First published in Great Britain by
HarperCollins *Children's Books* in 2019
Published in this edition in 2020
HarperCollins *Children's Books* is a division of HarperCollins*Publishers* Ltd,
HarperCollins Publishers
1 London Bridge Street
London SE1 9GF

The HarperCollins website address is:
www.harpercollins.co.uk

1

ISBN 978–0–00–826810–7

Sophy Henn asserts the moral right to be identified
as the author and illustrator of the work.

Typeset in New Clarendon 14/22pt by Goldy Broad
Printed and bound in China by RRD APS

MIX
Paper from
responsible sources
FSC™ C007454
FSC
www.fsc.org

This book is produced from independently certified FSC™ paper
to ensure responsible forest management.

For more information visit: www.harpercollins.co.uk/green

BAD Nana

ALL the FUN OF the FAiR

Sophy Henn

HarperCollins *Children's Books*

CONTENTS

Rockin'

THIS WAY UP

WHOOPEE

SECOND

J

My name is
Jeanie and I am 7 ¾.

My three favourite things
RIGHT NOW are fairy lights,
comics and milkshakes.
But NOT chocolate – EEEEWwWWw –
only vanilla or strawberry.

Oh, and of course I *still* like badges.
I can't even imagine
NOT liking them.

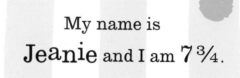

As I am only 7 ¾ I still live with my family. This is NOT ideal for many reasons and I really did *try* to **move** to the shed, but Dad said he couldn't find **anywhere** else to put the lawnmower, so THAT was the end of THAT.

My family is made up of my mum, my dad and my little brother, Jack, who really

tries his absolute best to annoy me ALL the time, but, as I am much, much older and much, much cleverer and much, much better than him, he actually doesn't bother me at all.

I do actually have LOTS of other family scattered about the place. We see them fairly often, usually after a really L O N G car journey packed full of Jack whining and moaning and smelling and whining and then getting in the way of my foot, which for some reason ends up with ME getting into trouble. This is extremely UNFAIR.

The relative we live closest to is **BAD NANA**.
She is one of my **three grandmas**,
which I know is one more than usual, but
Clare Coleman from school has **five**,
which is apparently really **great** for
birthdays and Christmas.

BAD NANA'S name isn't actually "BAD", and no one is exactly sure **when** or **why** or **who** started calling her that. But, if I was really, really, REALLY forced to guess who started it, I would guess my **dad**. He STILL moans about the balaclava **BAD NANA** knitted him one Christmas and that was almost one **million YEARS** ago.

I really think that was one of those times when Dad got "bad" and "fun" the wrong way round (he and Mum do that quite a lot) because **BAD NANA** is in actual fact a very brilliant person. And for lots of reasons, NOT just one. Here are some of those reasons:

- She always has biscuits.
- She always likes to have fun.
- She never gives you fruit for pudding.
- She always likes everyone else to have fun.
- She smells like sweets.
- She always has lemon sherbets.
- She is funny.
- She is a bit naughty sometimes but in a good way.

She always has a whoopee cushion in her handbag.

• AND if she is in a **super duper** double **good mood**, she will flick out her false teeth and **pretend** to be a **pirate**. (Only that is TOP SECRET and I am not supposed to talk about that.)

BAD NANA lives eight minutes and thirty-six seconds away (if you get a wiggle on) at 66 Broadbottom Road with *Liberace* her cat.

Liberace is pink, which is **extremely unusual** for a cat and might explain why he looks **surprised** all the time. Like he just saw what he looked like and instead of being a **normal** cat colour like black and white or tabby he is . . .

PINK! SURPRISE!

But, honestly, he has been pink for almost ALWAYS, so you would have thought it would be less surprising

by now.

BAD NANA is extremely **lucky** as all her friends seem to live on her road. They are called *Cynth*, *Sylv* and *Norman*, and those are just her **best friends**.

Very annoyingly, *my* best friends **don't** live on my road at all, but they are called Wilf, Marcy and Sukey. Sukey doesn't **even** live in our **town** anymore as she had to move away, but we still WRITE to each other and Mum says I can see her in the holidays, which I really **hope** is not just one of those things that **grown-ups** SAY and don't **actually** DO.

My brother, Jack, says he has **best friends** TOO, but I can't imagine it.

So **BAD NANA** is mainly up to her eyeballs in company, what with all that AND us. I spend a LOT of time at **BAD NANA'S** house on account of my mum and dad working AROUND THE CLOCK. And this is fine by me. What is less fine is that Jack has to spend a LOT of time at **BAD NANA'S** house too, and usually at the same time as me. I don't see why he can't just go to one of my other family members that lives a lot further away. Then he wouldn't

even need to come **home**
in between times – he could
just stay there.
FOREVER.

There is only one person **BAD NANA** really,
REALLY doesn't get on with, and that
is Mrs Farquar-Haha. **BAD NANA** says she
can't remember exactly how they became
such TOTAL enemies, but we have all
had the utter joy of seeing it in ACTION.*

* THAT was SARCASM. It's a new thing for me. But I quite liked the idea of it when Wilf explained it to me, so I thought I would give it a go. In case you don't know, it's saying the exact **opposite** of what you **mean**. It can be a risky business, but, so far, it has worked out okay.

My teacher, Mrs Fitzpatrick, says we can ALL get along if we try our **best** and that is a **nice** idea, but I am not sure Mrs Fitzpatrick has met **BAD NANA** and Mrs Farquar-Haha. Maybe they DON'T get along because they are almost **completely opposite** . . .

FUNNY

SILLY

GIGGLY

NAUGHTY

NOT VERY GOOD AT BEING BOSSED ABOUT

NOT AT ALL BEIGE

SMELLS LIKE SWEETS

LIKES CUPS OF TEA AND FUDGE

Mrs Farquar-Haha is almost ALL the things BAD NANA isn't keen on and BAD NANA is nearly EVERYTHING Mrs Farquar-Haha is NOT at all fond of. I have drawn a diagram to show this. It is a Venn diagram (we just did them in Maths).

SNOOTY

SHOUTY   BOSSY

SNOBBY   SCARY

WEARS ONLY BEIGE CLOTHES

SMELLS LIKE
TALCUM POWDER

HAS ZERO SENSE
OF HUMOUR

This would all be fine by me if it wasn't for the fact that Mrs Farquar-Haha's granddaughter, Georgina, has decided to NOT LIKE me as much as Mrs Farquar-Haha doesn't like **BAD NANA**. And this wouldn't even be SO bad if we weren't **stuck** together in a room EVERY SINGLE DAY (except weekends, thank heavens) because we are in the same class at school, which gives Georgina

PLENTY of time to find **new** and **embarrassing** ways to tease me.

Even with so many **other people** at school, and so much going on ALL the time, she NEVER misses a single *slightly* NOT ORDINARY thing I do, or any chance to let me know how much **better** she is **than me** at stuff. In fact, Georgina thinks she's NUMBER ONE at pretty much **everything**.

BEE NICE

POPCORN

ACE

SUPER STAR

FAIRLY EXCITING

FRIENDS 4 EVER

It was very nearly **town fair day** and we were all u^{p}s^{i}de d$_o$w$_n$ with excitement. This is because there is only ONE town fair day in a **whole** year, so you really, really look forward to it, and also because there is MASSES of stuff going on and nearly all of the stuff is BRILLIANT. It isn't like a funfair – although there is a **biggish**

wheel – it's the other type of fair with lots of stalls and sweets and shows and sweets and games and sweets.

Everything happens down on the common with all the stalls round the edge, and in the middle there's a roped-off SQUARE, which for some reason is called a ring. I honestly don't know why because it's a square – anyone can see that, *even* Ryan Higgins and he would be the first to say that Maths isn't his best subject.

Anyway, all through the whole entire fair there is stuff going on in the SQUARE ring like shows or dancing or displays or competitions . . .

In actual fact, there are a LOT of competitions at the town fair, like

the fancy-dress competition,

the pet-show competition,

the flower-arranging competition,

the giant-vegetable competition,

a whole LOAD of craft competitions and the grand finale –

the BAKE-A-RAMA!

– which is really just a cake competition. I quite like there being loads of competitions because wherever there is a competition there is *usually* a prize, unless it's a JUST-FOR-THE-FUN-OF-IT competition, which is okay, but prizes are a little bit more okay-er.

Wilf, Marcy and me had decided to enter only ONE of the competitions **each** because we wanted to give everyone else a **chance** too. We all had our eyes on a prize and the prize I had **my** eyes on was a hugely **ginormous** teddy bear, which was the FIRST-PRIZE prize in the fancy-dress competition. As I had a **brilliant** idea for a costume, I was feeling quite a bit **confident** and had *even* given the hugely **ginormous** teddy bear a NAME. TERRY. On account of him looking like a **Terry**.

It had taken quite a LONG time for me to think of my **brilliant** costume idea, and in the end it wasn't even just my thinking that thought of it. I thought about it all through Maths, which was a **mistake** as

I accidentally answered "sausage dog" when Mr Workman asked me what 12 x 12 was, because that was my first good idea. But then I realised I might not get noticed, being so FLAT on the ground . . .

Then I thought about
going as a dinosaur
because they are extremely
NOTICEABLE, but then I thought
my costume would probably be so good
it might actually SCARE lots of small
children at the competition and, although
that would increase my chances,
I DIDN'T really want to do that.

Then I rummaged through my wardrobe and found my lost lucky sock and an old gobstopper and about a million hairbands and my rubber-band ball and my key-ring collection and a strawberry lip balm, but MOST IMPORTANTLY I found my old purple gymnastics leotard. It was quite a bit TOO SMALL for me, but I had kept it JUST IN CASE it might come in handy some time, and it felt like that time might be now o'clock.

But even though I thought about it all through a whole Assembly I had NO IDEA how to make it into a prize-winning fancy-dress costume, so I took it with me to BAD NANA'S because she is actually full of ideas as she is so super old and has had aaaaages to think of them all.

And obviously **BAD NANA** had the best idea EVER . . . She said I should wear the old purple gymnastics leotard, my navy school tights (the good ones without any holes) and then fix LOTS of balloons to me and go as a bunch of grapes! TA-DA!

I cut some leaves out of green paper for extra-special real-life detail and BAD NANA helped me stick them to a hair band. It looked terrific and I was SO excited about my costume that I felt fidgety every time I thought about it. I was positive I was in with a good chance and I even worked out how I would fit my hugely ginormous teddy bear Terry into my room. (Get rid of the wardrobe.)

I COULD.
NOT.
WAIT.

Double annoyingly, my brother, Jack, is a complete and TOTAL copycat and can't think of ANY of his own ideas so he said he was going to enter the fancy-dress competition too. He even told us he was going to wear a cardboard box and go as a parcel.

I think this REALLY definitely scientifically PROVES that if you only eat cheese puffs and watch survival programmes your brain STOPS working properly and you can only think of rubbish ideas. I might write to the NEWS about it.

Marcy had decided to enter her hamster, Peanut, into the pet show and we were all extremely CERTAIN that Peanut had a really GOOD chance as he is definitely the cutest hamster we know. He is also the only hamster we know, but that does NOT stop him from being super cute. Marcy told us she was brushing Peanut every single day with a TINY brush she borrowed from her brother's Little Pony set, so his fur would be super shiny and tangle free for the competition. We all agreed this could only help his chances of winning BEST SMALL PET.

Jack and I thought **BAD NANA** should enter 𝓛𝓲𝓫𝓮𝓻𝓪𝓬𝓮 into the pet show and we checked the categories, but unfortunately there wasn't one for MOST SURPRISED PET.

This was a big shame as 𝓛𝓲𝓫𝓮𝓻𝓪𝓬𝓮 would definitely have WON, what with surprised being his favourite and ONLY expression. Maggie in the dress shop's pug, SPANGLES, would definitely have come a close SECOND, though.

2ND

Wilf decided to have a go at **winning** a prize because he said he might as well have something to do while Marcy and I talked about our prize-winning plans NON-STOP! But as Wilf had **no pet** and wasn't **keen** on dressing up he decided to make a **garden** in a baking tray, which is actually a CATEGORY in the **craft**

section of the competitions. Jack said that was impossible as baking trays are QUITE SMALL and gardens are quite a bit BIGGER, so Wilf had to explain that actually it is a shrunk-down garden and the plants can be made from plasticine. Jack said he understood, but I'm NOT so sure.

We had ALL gone so **competition bonkers** that *even* Dad had decided to enter the BAKE-A-RAMA. He said it was **selfish** of him to **deny** the judges the chance to taste his coffee-and-walnut cake.

This **confused** me as I thought NOT making the judges eat his coffee-and-walnut cake would be the **nicest** thing he could do, because there is only ONE thing I don't like more than the taste of **coffee** and THAT is the taste of **walnuts**. But, really, I've had it up to my ARMPITS with **bunting** and **baking**.

CHILLI
BEANS

STINKY
SMELLY

BATH
SALTS

SMELL

AH 897120
498

RDIAL

AH 886350
499

ORANGE BIT

Mum was running the TOMBOLA, which is actually a complete puzzle to me and I cannot work out why people would spend REAL money on the chance to win prizes like talc or bars of soap or tins of soup. Surely prizes should be all EXCITING and prizey? Like sweets or badges or ginormous teddy bears or sweets!

YUMMY HONEY

PEAS

MUSHY SOUP

QUITE **NICE** BISCUITS

Anyway, with ALL the
costumes and plasticine plants,
hamster-brushing, shopping
for coffee and walnuts and
boring tombola prizes,
we were all as BUSY as
really, **really** busy bees.
It was EXHAUSTING.

SQUASH

JAM

BEANZ
BEANZ
BEANZ

TUFF

TH
LTS

sweet money

HAPPY DAYS

YAY

Actual, actual fair day

After about a
hundred years
of extremely BUSY waiting,
it was finally town fair day.

WAAAAHHHHOOOOOOO!

I jumped out of bed as soon as I woke up
and I charged downstairs and gobbled
some breakfast *SUPER FAST* as there was
a LOT to do. Then I realised it was still
dark and still night and everyone was
still asleep, so I went back to bed and
did it all AGAIN a few hours later when
it was actually daylight and,
in fact, the morning.

BAD NANA arrived when everyone was finally up and about, which meant we could all get busy planning our action-packed day. This mainly involved Mum lining us up and telling us EXACTLY what was happening and when it was happening and where we should be while it was happening.

There was SO much happening that my brain slightly STOPPED listening, but I think I got the general gist.

I packed my fancy-dress costume into my PE bag, taking extra-special care over my leafy headband, which now had grapevines made of pipe cleaners for extra-special detail. Sukey had sent them to me for GOOD LUCK, and I really did feel a bit luckier for having them.

As the car was COMPLETELY full of my mum and my dad and extremely unexciting TOMBOLA prizes and a gazebo and camping chairs and coffee-and-walnut cake, BAD NANA, Jack and me had to walk to the common using our feet. It took us soooo *LONG*, what with Jack being soooooo SLOW, and I was so itching to get there that it ACTUALLY felt like we were walking in slow motion.

When we FINALLY arrived at the common everything was where it was supposed to be, so we found Mum at the TOMBOLA stall really easily.

You could smell all the double yummy smells of SWEETS and candyfloss and hotdogs and fun and SWEETS and prize-winning possibilities. Mmmᵐᵐₘₘₘm!

I almost **popped** with EXCITEMENT when I saw Wilf and Marcy heading over with Marcy's mum. Wilf's mum and dad have to work on Saturdays and Marcy's mum is up to her **nostrils** with ALLLLL of Marcy's baby brothers and sisters, so **BAD NANA** was **in charge** and we were **happy** about that.

Marcy had brought Peanut, her very possibly **prize-winning** hamster, with her, and her little brother had let her bring his *Little Pony* hair brush for any last-minute grooming. That must be what it's

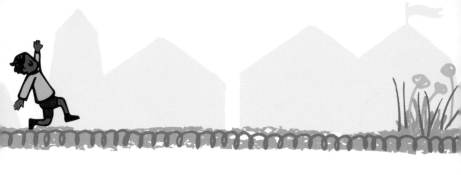

like to have a NICE and **kind** little brother
instead of a **smelly** and ANNOYING one.

Peanut was snuggled up inside his
little **mobile home,** and Marcy said it
was really great to be able USE it as
Peanut doesn't really need to go anywhere
normally. And I had a little **think** about
where a hamster might
need to go, and she was
RIGHT, not really
anywhere.

Right then the local marching band started playing, and marched across the common to the SQUARE ring with purpose. The marching band is ¾ Braithwaite family (we've been doing fractions in Maths too) and I sometimes wonder if they ever wear their uniforms when they aren't marching, like at family get-togethers. I know I definitely would if I was them because there is

lots and LOTS of stuff on their uniforms like fringy bits and shiny buttons and bits of gold rope. But you could ONLY wear them on special occasions as they are just TOO fancy for everyday. Mum took a short break from TOMBOLA business to giggle at the xylophone – it's just the sound apparently. Grown-ups can be completely ridiculous sometimes. It's really very confusing.

Mrs Farquar-Haha was MARCHING precisely one split second behind them, but NOT in a fun way, and she didn't have any fancy rope bits on her outfit. What she DID have was a giant clipboard, megaphone and a HUGE rosette that said HEAD JUDGE on it, because she was probably going to need to make notes VERY LOUDLY as she was chief of ALL the judges. She was actually looking *FURIOUS* . . .

which seemed strange to me as I would have imagined that SHOUTING ORDERS and judging people are her very favourite things to do. And she was in for a WHOLE day of doing just THAT.

The big loud-speaker system, which they use during the fair for letting people know when things are happening or if any lost things/ children have been handed in or even who has won the raffle or other stuff like that, crickled and crackled and the announcer man announced the fair was OPEN. My tummy did a little flip as I thought of ALL the brilliant things we were going to do and the prizes we might WIN . . .

THE
CAT'S
WHISKERS

CLOUD
9

'small but
MIGHTY

I ♥
DOGS

A GOOD
SIGN

IT'S
(Pet)
SHOWTIME

I ♥ CATS

Hi!

The FIRST thing first was the pet show and this was a good job too as Peanut couldn't be out and about ALL DAY LONG – he's only a tiny hamster. Me and Marcy and Peanut and Wilf and Jack and BAD NANA all headed to the SQUARE ring on account of Mrs Farquar-Haha SHOUTING into her megaphone that the pet show was about to START NOW. She actually shouted so loudly that her megaphone made some ROBOT shrieking noises and Buttons, Emma Parker's little dog, got so scared he hid his tail in between his legs.

This was especially NOT good as he was entering the PET with the WAGGIEST TAIL category. Not even a snippet of cheese would make him wag his tail, and Emma said cheese is his absolute favourite.

BAD NANA told us she had decided NOT to enter Liberace in the pet show on account of him finding it all just TOO surprising, which I think was absolutely the right decision.

All the pets that had entered looked really lovely and smart; Andrew Higgins had even tied a **ribbon** round his goldfish's bowl. About the EXACT time I was thinking how lovely it all was, Georgina Farquar-Haha came hurtling into the SQUARE ring with a giant golden retriever and sent everyone

FLYING. Now, I like golden retrievers a LOT – in actual fact, I would *even* say there is NOT a dog I DON'T like, and this golden retriever's name is Monty, which everyone knows is an extremely good dog name. What I WASN'T so keen on was the fact that this golden retriever belonged to Mrs Farquar-Haha, the EXACT same Mrs Farquar-Haha who was judging the competition, and that DIDN'T seem *quite* right.

Once everyone had settled down from the Georgina and Monty-sized kerfuffle, they all lined up in the SQUARE ring with their pets. Mrs Farquar-Haha stood in FRONT of the line and barked out different categories. When she barked out

your pet's category you had to step forward with your pet, and stay there until she had judged you both. It felt extremely serious and NOT much like fun, and even the pets seemed to look a bit scared, all except for Monty.

If I am **completely** honest, Mrs Farquar-Haha DIDN'T seem to **like** ANY of the pets other than Monty.

She frowned at Bubbles the goldfish, she sneered at Buster the bunny, she *barely* even noticed Peanut and his super-shiny tangle-free coat, and I don't actually know how to describe the face she pulled when Martin Watson opened his matchbox to show her Chuckles, his pet earwig. But I do know it WASN'T a happy face. Even Sarah James's little dog, the Colonel, didn't *even* get a smile from Mrs Farquar-Haha and he can dance on his back legs. (Only for treats, though. He's NOT an idiot.)

Everyone and their pet seemed to get quite a bit nervous. Gary, Charlotte Hopkins's toy poodle, must have been extra nervous because he even did a little wee.

After all the barking – Mrs Farquar-Haha's, NOT the dogs (they were actually **all very nice**) – the RESULTS were announced, and Peanut didn't *quite* win the BEST SMALL PET because Twinkle, Clare Hargreaves's guinea pig, won that. But Peanut **did** come an extremely close **second**, which was

brilliant and it didn't matter that there were only TWO pets in that category: second is **second**.

There were **nearly** three entrants as Jack made a last-minute bid to enter the BEST SMALL PET category as he told us he was **sure** he had **nits** and they are small and if he gives them **names** surely that makes them **pets**? **BAD NANA** told him to keep quiet and we all started to s͜c͜r͜a͜t͜c͜h our heads. Nitwit!

After the BEST SMALL PET was announced, it was time for PET with the WAGGIEST TAIL and other than Buttons, whose tail suggested he was still very SCARED of Mrs Farquar-Haha, all the pets with tails were wagging away like crazy, even Ginny James's cat Mittens! They all did really well, but I don't think any of us were **completely surprised** when Mrs Farquar-Haha announced **Monty** was the **winner**.

To be fair to Monty, his tail was the **waggiest**, but then I suppose that would be the case when your real-life **owner** is the judge and you are **actually** pleased to see them, *even* if they are Mrs Farquar-Haha.

But we were a little bit **surprised** when he also won SMILIEST PET . . .

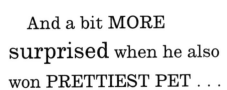

And a bit MORE **surprised** when he also won PRETTIEST PET . . .

And we were actually *quite* **startled** when he won BEST-DRESSED PET as well (especially as he was **only** wearing a **collar** and Barry Bates had dressed his cat, Harry, up as a **wizard**) . . .

And you could have knocked us over with a **feather** when he won SMARTEST PET . . .

But by the time it came for Mrs Farquar-Haha to announce BEST IN SHOW we had **stopped** being quite so surprised and sort of **expected** Monty to WIN. Which he did. Unsurprisingly.

By now **BAD NANA** was not just completely unsurprised about ALL of Monty's wins – I could tell she was also pretty pipped about them too. Her face had gone a mild shade of pink and her good beady eye was fixed right on Mrs Farquar-Haha, even while she was sneaking all the other human contestants a lemon sherbet for just having a go.

I felt a bit awful for Monty as he clearly had NO idea what was going on at all (a solid reason why he should NOT have won SMARTEST PET) and he hadn't even had a sniff of a rosette as Georgina had grabbed them ALL up and was wearing them all over her with a smile that made her look like she was in an advert and had just had some very tasty yoghurt.

Anyway, we all agreed that Peanut seemed to really enjoy getting out and about in his mobile home and all made a pinkie promise to have a think about more places to take him out and about in the future.

After all that **excitement**, we found Marcy's mum, who looked a bit like she'd had enough of town fair day, even though it had only really been going for half an hour. We handed her Peanut so she could have **one more** thing to keep an eye on, on the way home.

Then, after a suspiciously **good** rummage in her **ginormous** handbag, **BAD NANA** announced she was popping off to see the ANNOUNCER MAN who makes the announcements on the big speakers. When I asked her WHY, she said she had **found** something someone had **lost** and was going to hand it in. Then I wondered what on earth she was on about as she'd seemed too busy being **pipped** at Mrs Farquar-Haha to have the time to find anything.

I didn't have to **wonder** for very long . . .
Just as soon as she returned, the big
speakers crickled and crackled and
the man who makes the announcements
ANNOUNCED that . . .

Somebody has handed
that they think might
Has a Mrs Farquar-Haha

in some lost marbles

belong to a Mrs Farquar-Haha.

LOST HER MARBLES?

All of us FROZE completely STILL, even Peanut. Only **BAD NANA** made a noise, which sounded just like a giggle, but she swore was actually a SNEEZE. (It wasn't.) I think we all stood soooo still as we knew something was about to happen, but weren't sure exactly what. About a nanosecond later, we were in fact quite sure because we heard a noise like a tweed volcano ERUPTING, and then Mrs Farquar-Haha stormed out of the SQUARE ring and straight over to the announcer man who makes the announcements, and we all agreed that he was quite probably DONE FOR.

It turned out that Mrs Farquar-Haha didn't really need a megaphone as we could all very clearly hear EXACTLY what she thought of the announcer man who makes the announcements. He tried to point out that he was only announcing things people **told him** to announce, but she didn't seem to be able to HEAR him over her own shouting.

tiNY GReeN FiNGeRs

YOU GOT THIS!

Once we had **stopped** hearing Mrs Farquar-Haha SHOUTING, we realised that it was almost time for Wilf's BAKING-TRAY garden competition, but not quite. So we all popped in a lemon sherbet and wandered over to the SQUARE ring just in time for the *twirling* display.

This was SUPER lucky because the *twirlers* were really, really, really brilliant and SUPER amazing, but then they always are. Wilf and I were SO excited when they ran into the SQUARE ring while

pointing their toes at the same time because we really do want to be *twirlers* when we're a bit bigger.

Marcy isn't so keen as she gets car sick really easily and she told us that if she had to do a *super quick turn* she would probably throw up. But I think mainly it's because she's NOT a big fan of sparkly leotards, which is an essential part of *twirling*. I would rather sparkly dungarees if I am really honest, but they DON'T seem to wear those.

Anyway I think the *twirlers* were as super excited as me and Wilf because one of them *twirled* so *FAST* and threw her baton UP with such *twirl* power that she FELL straight over and her baton got stuck up in the tree. We all felt really sorry for her *especially* when we saw Georgina laughing and pointing, which is EXACTLY what she likes to do when someone does something they didn't quite mean to.

The *twirler* looked really quite upset, but she carried on anyway and did the the WHOLE routine without her baton at all and honestly you would hardly have actually noticed. Wilf and I agreed that she was super professional and that when we are *twirlers* that is EXACTLY what we will do if our batons ever got stuck up a tree.

After all that, we only had time to hook just the one duck before we had to go and find the CRAFT tent for Wilf's BAKING-TRAY garden competition. Wilf was a bit worried we would be LATE, but he needn't have been because the craft tent was extremely easy to find as it was quite a BIG tent with CRAFT written above it in GIANT letters, which helped. BAD NANA and Wilf filled out the little entry form and we all wished his garden GOOD LUCK. Wilf had to put his garden on a long table and stand behind it, like ALL the other people who had entered

the competition. It turned out we knew some of the other entrants too . . . Freddie, Lydia (who mainly walks on tiptoes) and Billy Gibson whose garden was less gardeny and more FOOTBALL PITCHY, but then he really loves football so it actually made a LOT of sense. There was a whole gaggle of judges for this competition and they were in a huddle, probably discussing what makes a good baking-tray garden a GREAT baking-tray garden.

Just as we were giving Wilf the thumbs up, Mrs Farquar-Haha popped out of the middle of the judges' huddle, looking FURIOUS. Our thumbs drooped a little bit when we saw her because this reminded us she was the tip-top judge of ALL the judges. But Marcy pointed out that at least Georgina or Monty HADN'T entered the baking-tray garden competition, so Wilf was STILL in with a good chance.

It turned out Marcy had spoken TOO soon because just at that very minute Georgina MARCHED IN, still covered in Monty's rosettes plus some new ones. She barged right into the middle of the line and put her baking-tray garden (which seemed to be ninety per cent stones and NOT much garden) down on the table. Even though Monty HADN'T entered the competition, it still felt like Wilf's chances might NOT be *quite* as good now, but we smiled our biggest and best GOOD-LUCK SMILES anyway and the judging began.

It was **extremely** nerve-racking, what with Mrs Farquar-Haha walking **up** and **down** the table with her clipboard, trying to look all IMPORTANT, but mainly looking like she could **smell** something and that the **something** she could smell **smelt** really, REALLY **bad**. Most of the other judges walked along behind her **nodding**, like they could smell it TOO and agreed that it WAS a **bad smell**.

Wilf looked **proud** of his garden as he stood in line and this was absolutely how he SHOULD have looked because his garden was really very brilliant. I strongly felt that we should show our appreciation for all his hard work, but it DIDN'T really seem like a **cheering** or **clapping** situation, so me and Marcy and **BAD NANA** and Jack all MIMED cheering instead, which I think was *quite* helpful.

After precisely hardly ANY time at all, Mrs Farquar-Haha got back into the huddle with her fellow judges and they had an EXTREMELY short conversation. From what I could make out it looked

like Mrs Farquar-Haha said something and they all **nodded**, EXCEPT Mr Cuthbert, who runs the local baker's – he just **rolled** his eyes – but Mrs Farquar-Haha GLARED at him and then his eyes

just

looked

at

the

FLOOR.

Everything got even more tense and if we had been sitting down we would definitely have been on the EDGE of our seats. I even started to hum 'La Cucaracha' without even realising, and even FASTER than the speeded-up marching band version, so I could hardly even keep up with myself. It was so SUPER lucky BAD NANA put a reassuring hand on my shoulder and I STOPPED humming before Georgina could notice. The LAST thing I needed was ANOTHER silly nickname from her (current nickname – Screamie Jeanie). Then it was time for Mrs Farquar-Haha to announce the winners.

She stood in front of the tables and said something very *quickly* about how great everyone's gardens were and did a LITTLE smile with her mouth that the rest of her face DIDN'T know about. Then she announced that someone called Katie, who had made a very impressive vegetable patch, was FOURTH, Lydia who mainly walks on tiptoes was THIRD, and then she did a reaaaaaallly long dramatic pause like they do on the telly – it went on for AGGGGGGGES – and then

Wilf was SECOND and that the very best garden by FAR had won and that the winner was Georgina, with her MINIATURE rockery. I felt BAD NANA'S reassuring hand start to GRIP my shoulder tighter and tighter and it was almost hurting when I wriggled FREE. BAD NANA apologised and said she DIDN'T realise what she was doing and she said all of this while NOT

looking at me at all but STRAIGHT at Mrs Farquar-Haha with her good beady eye NARROWED soooo much I wasn't even sure she could actually SEE out of it. Her face was now quite extremely pink, and that meant she was either almost at FULL pip or being in the hot tent had got to her. Either way, it wasn't GOOD.

Georgina grabbed her rosette and barged out of the tent, saying something about having to go and win ANOTHER competition like it was the most boring thing the whole world. Wilf and Lydia and the Vegetable Patch

person all got THEIR rosettes and we all clapped and said WELL DONE and it was mainly great and, even though something felt a little bit WRONG, no one said anything because it wasn't really that sort of moment.

When we finally got OUT of the tent and **BAD NANA** was less than bright pink, we saw that there was another show in the SQUARE ring, because the show really did in actual fact HAVE to go on. If you had told me the thing that was going to cheer me up was the

local synchronised-swimming team, I am not sure I would have **believed** you. But they really did put on an excellent display, even WITHOUT a swimming pool . . . It was SO good Marcy even thought she might start doing that while Wilf and I are being *twirlers*.

BAD NANA said she had to just pop off for a second and we were to stay EXACTLY where we were – AGAIN! This wasn't a problem as it felt like the synchronised swimmers were building up to a very BIG finish. We did slightly wonder why **BAD NANA** was walking towards the announcer man who makes the ANNOUNCEMENTS again, and why when she spoke to him they both started giggling, but then Penny Heard's mum did a dry-land UPSIDE-DOWN twirl and we stopped wondering and carried on watching the display.

BAD NANA finally came back to the SQUARE ring with a bit of a giggle still on her face. Then the loud speakers crickled and crackled and the announcer man who makes the ANNOUNCEMENTS announced that the very first RAFFLE winner of the day had been picked aaaaand . . .

CONGRATULATIONS to Mrs Farquar-Hah

Very Big Humongous Frilly Pants from th

Could she please come and make herself know

Ver

ho has won a lifetime's supply of

ery-Big-Humongous-Frilly-Pants Stall.

the new owner and winning wearer of

Big Humongous Frilly Pants.

This time the whole fair seemed to

F R E E Z E,

except for one super *FAST*,

extremely LOUD

and very

ANGRY

Mrs Farquar-Haha,

who sort of *ZOOMED* across the fair

from one side to the other.

She

STOMPED

through the

hook-a-duck

pool . . .

she BOINGED across the bouncy castle

and she DIDN'T even seem to care who she sent F$_L$Y$_I$N$_G$ through the tea tent.

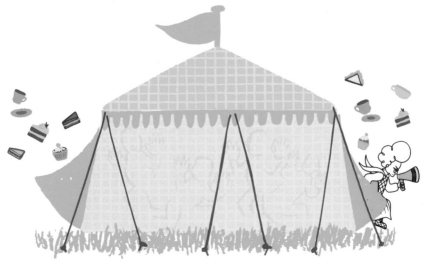

119

By the time she reached the announcer man it was *almost* as if flames were SHOOTING OUT behind her and she was an **ANGRY** rocket and, just like a rocket, angry or NOT, she sort of EXPLODED in front of the announcing man, who this time had sensibly put some **headphones** on to cushion his ears from her **very LOUD** *SCREECHING*. And they must have worked because he was just **smiling** at her like he couldn't even **hear** all the MEAN things she was saying, which actually seemed to make her

EXPLODE
even
more.

I looked at **BAD NANA** with one of my "Was this anything to do with you?" looks (I learned it from Mum), but she didn't notice as she was suddenly CONCENTRATING ever so much on the synchronised-swimming show.

I honestly meant to keep asking her, but then I got distracted by the synchronised swimmers' FINALE, which really was quite spectacular.

We were all enjoying it so much that we very nearly forgot the time completely. In fact, if I'm honest, I DID forget the time and I think Marcy and Wilf and Jack did too, but BAD NANA DIDN'T, and that was a good job because I had a ginormous teddy bear called Terry to win.

†HANKS a BUNCH

BEAR
WITH
ME

ME

TERRY

POP!

I had to get changed behind the TOMBOLA stall, which WASN'T ideal as there was still quite a queue. BAD NANA and Jack held up a blanket for me to get changed behind, so it WASN'T completely embarrassing, just a bit. Wilf, Marcy and Dad helped with the balloon blowing-up. BAD NANA said Dad was

full of HOT AIR so that would be NO problemo for him. Mum even took a bit of a break from all the tombola madness and safety-pinned the balloons to me. There was a slightly worrying moment when it looked as if I might NOT be able to actually walk, and Mum had to take some balloons/grapes off. But it all worked out okay in the end.

Everyone offered to help Jack too, but he said he was fine as he had made TWO straps from sticky tape, and stuck a label on the FRONT of the cardboard box he was wearing which said "To Jack". I asked him why he was sending himself to himself and he asked me why I was the most annoying sister in the whole world and I said THANK YOU but I didn't think we had time to list all my super skills and then he stuck his tongue out and Mum told us both to

KNOCK
IT
OFF.

So we did.

I was COMPLETELY boiling by the time I got to the SQUARE ring as it turns out wearing balloons and tights and a slightly too-small leotard altogether makes you VERY hot, but there was no time to really think about that as

Mrs Farquar-Haha was SHRIEKING into her completely unnecessary MEGAPHONE that it was time for the fancy-dress competition . . .

NOW! NOW! NOW!

I straightened my leafy headband and wonkied the pipe-cleaner viney bits while the SQUARE ring filled up with dinosaurs, vampires, footballers, loads of princesses, a couple of spidermen and a punk, AND ALL SORTS!

Other than being a bit melty, I was still feeling really good about my costume, and STRONGLY felt I was in with a good chance of leaving with the ginormous teddy bear called Terry. I spotted Betsy Barton and hopped over to say hello. I would normally give Betsy a hug, but the grapes got in the way so we waved at each other instead. Betsy was dressed as a dog, and even if you only *slightly* know Betsy this would come as no surprise because she is MAD about dogs. Barking mad! She actually likes them so much that one lunchtime she REFUSED to speak in proper words and would only bark or yap until the bell went. Anyway, we were having a great chat (in words not barks this time) about what an extremely exciting day town fair day is when SUDDENLY the balloon static from my grapes started to do strange things to the fur on Betsy's Dalmatian costume so I scooted back to BAD NANA before we got ELECTRIC SHOCKS and our hair went on end, like in Science.

Of course, just as the competition was about to start, Georgina came *RUNNING* into the SQUARE ring dressed as a wedding princess. I really didn't want it to, as it felt a bit mean, but my heart S_{A_NK} a little bit as it did seem like she was winning every single competition EVER. To keep my spirits up, I tried to think of the ginormous teddy bear called Terry who very probably

WANTED to live with me and that sort of did the trick. Then we all had to line up **alphabetically**, which meant I had to stand next to Penny Heard. I wouldn't mind **normally** because I really like Penny Heard – sometimes we even do skipping together – but right then Penny Heard was dressed up as a SPIKY hedgehog and as I was covered in balloons this felt a little bit **worrying**.

It turned out I was spot on to be a bit worried as when the judges told us to scooch up – so we would all fit in one long line – the WORST THING happened and Penny Heard's hedgehog SPIKES popped a couple of my grapes and made TWO really LOUD BANGS. It was a TOTAL costume disaster, but that

BANG!

BANG!

wasn't even the WORST part. The worst part was that Mrs Farquar-Haha's prize-winning dog, Monty, was there and you would never imagine it because he lives with Mrs Farquar-Haha, but he is actually very scared of LOUD noises. So when the grapes/balloons popped he *RAN OFF* under the plant stall and it took a good half an hour and a bit of the Lord Mayor's sausage roll to get him out again.

Even though it was NOT actually my fault that ANY of that happened, Mrs Farquar-Haha seemed to think otherwise. Once Monty was safely OUT from under the stall and back to his normal waggy self, she TOWERED over me and as she looked down her beaky nose, shooting *LIGHTNING BOLTS* out of her eyeballs, she told me I was quite possibly the WORST example of fancy dress she had had the misfortune to judge during her long, long, loooong time of judging EVERYTHING. She said I had clearly NOT made any sort of effort and there was even a hole in my tights, which I felt was very UNFAIR as, other than accidentally getting my tights in a muddle, I had really made a huge lot of effort.

Then she lifted up her MEGAPHONE and aimed it right in my face as she boomed at me that I was DISQUALIFIED from the competition for health and safety reasons, and that I must leave the ring . . .

RIGHT NOW!

I tried to tell her it was actually a SQUARE and that I was really, REALLY sorry if Monty was upset and that I hadn't meant to wear my holey tights and that I really had made an effort, but before I could say anything she turned up the MEGAPHONE to max and snarled . . .

IMMEDIATELY!

This WASN'T at all how I thought the fancy-dress competition would turn out, and what with THAT and the worry about Monty and the disappointment of not even *slightly* winning first prize and the certain knowledge that Georgina would tease me about this FOREVER, I got a bit upset. Then, when I realised I was about to cry in front of everyone AND while I was dressed as a bunch of grapes, I hid in amongst my grape balloons as much as I could, and I got a bit MORE upset.

And just when I COULDN'T imagine ever NOT feeling upset again BAD NANA appeared by my side and held my hand, which IMMEDIATELY made me feel a smidge bit better. I even *peeked* out from my grape balloons and saw BAD NANA raise herself up to her FULL HEIGHT of 4ft 10" and possibly also go on her tiptoes, so she could almost look Mrs Farquar-Haha RIGHT in the chin. She was clearly EXTREMELY pipped, and in her IMPORTANT voice, which she usually saves for talking on the phone, BAD NANA told Mrs Farquar-Haha that it would NOT be necessary to disqualify me as, even though I was the best bunch of grapes this fancy-dress competition had ever seen, I was retiring from the competition IMMEDIATELY due to one of the judges having ANGER issues.

Well, I think we ALL knew which judge she was talking about, and even Georgina LAUGHED at this until Mrs Farquar-Haha fixed her with the stink eye. Then BAD NANA and me turned around and walked out of the SQUARE ring. And although I was very disappointed NOT to win the ginormous teddy bear called Terry or in fact ANY prize at all, and despite being quite sad that my grapes had not *even* been given a bit of a chance, and even though I was still very embarrassed at being SHOUTED AT in front of THE WHOLE FAIR, holding tightly on to BAD NANA'S hand made me feel a bit like everything would be ALL RIGHT, and I managed to come out from hiding in my grape/balloons completely. We were actually making quite a DRAMATIC exit until one of my remaining grape/balloons came loose and made a LONG, whiny, sad *RASPBERRY NOISE.*

Still, it could have been worse.

Maybe.

It surprised **exactly** NO ONE at all that Georgina came FIRST in the fancy-dress competition, and I felt so **sorry** for the poor **ginormous** teddy bear called Terry as he would have to **live** with **her** now and she probably DIDN'T

even know his name was Terry. Penny Heard came SECOND, which felt quite unfair as everyone could see an actual homemade hedgehog is quite a bit MORE interesting than a wedding princess, which is JUST a princess but in white. A superhero came THIRD and that was that. It all felt so upside down that I was *even* SAD for Jack NOT winning anything, and then I felt MORE upside down because I NEVER feel sad for Jack.

We met Wilf and Marcy over at the tombola stall and they gave me as much of a hug as they could, which wasn't much as I still had most of my balloon grapes on, but it made me feel MUCH better. I knew they understood exactly how I felt. We weren't sad for NOT winning our competitions, more for NOT even having a chance. It didn't feel like town fair day, more like town UNFAIR day. It's really quite annoying when grown-ups tell YOU to play fair and everything, but then THEY go and DO the opposite THEMSELVES. Annoying, confusing and extremely VERY annoying.

Just when we **almost** felt okay again,
Georgina and Mrs Farquar-Haha walked
over and **BAD NANA** made a funny gurgling
noise. Georgina started saying how
sorry she was about my grapes popping
and that I mustn't be **TOO** disappointed
as it was really about the **taking part**,
which is very **easy** to **say** when you
are completely **COVERED** in **winning**.
I tried **really** hard **NOT** to look upset
while she said this because of course she
was **RIGHT**, but I wasn't at all **sure** what

to do with my **face** because Georgina has never ACTUALLY been **nice** to me. EVER. But before I could work it out she went right back to **normal** and told me that being DISQUALIFIED must at least make a nice **change** from being a LOSER. Then she and Mrs Farquar-Haha *DASHED OFF* on account of her dance group *Glitter Bugz* doing a display in the SQUARE ring and needing plenty of time to put on enough **hairspray** to stop their hair budging one SINGLE millimetre.

We all sort of looked at our feet, then each other, then BACK at our feet because it really was one of those moments where you cannot think of a single thing to say.

BAD NANA was silent TOO, but the sort of silent that is REALLY loud. I even popped to the tombola stall, got changed, popped back and she was still being noisily quiet. Then she popped in a lemon sherbet, CRUNCHED it very loudly and I could tell she was having a THINK, all while she went at least TWO shades pinker. It was extremely clear she had gone to PIP LEVEL 11 (which is ONE more than FULL PIP) and that could only mean

ONE
THING . . .

TROUBLE!

All eyes were on **BAD NANA** and we were all braced for goodness knows what, but then – and I don't think ANY of us saw this coming – she had a very *ENERGETIC* rummage in her handbag, smiled a TINY smile and told us she had to pop to the JAM stall and the CAKE stall and the TEA tent. And we were to stay exactly where we were until she came back, AGAIN!

Well, we couldn't stay exactly where we were as that was RIGHT in front of the tombola and, UNBELIEVABLY, people were still queueing for it, even though the only prizes left were soap and squash.

So we shuffled along a bit and waited there. We could still see the SQUARE ring, and the local belly-dancing group were all wiggling about all over the place. Mrs Carter was **wiggling** with such GUSTO that she had to be **helped off** HALFWAY through on account of belly-dancing her BACK out. But even though they were a belly down, it really DIDN'T spoil the overall effect at all.

Just as the OLDEN DAYS Re-enactment Society started their show, **BAD NANA** came back, looking a little bit like she might burst out laughing at any minute, which was quite the TURNAROUND, mood-wise, and gave me a very uneasy feeling. I put myself on HIGH ALERT for any mischief that might be about to happen and I WARNED Marcy and Wilf too, but NOT Jack because he just wouldn't understand.

I ♥ CAKE

BAKE OFF!

Bake-A-rama DraMa

The BIG speakers crickled and crackled and the announcer man who makes the announcements ANNOUNCED that the final competition of the day was about to begin in the TEA TENT – the

BAAAAAKE-AAAAAA-RAAAAMMMAAAAAA

That is exactly how he said it, which made me wonder if he'd had too many pink wafers as that exact thing happens to Jack if he eats more than THREE

in under TEN minutes. I wasn't too sure I could bear **another** competition, but I wanted to support Dad, and **BAD NANA** was suddenly very enthusiastic about cake, so we all bundled into the tent. I saw Cynth, **BAD NANA'S** best, best friend, who was also in charge of the TEA TENT. I waved at her and she waved back and then she winked at **BAD NANA** and **BAD NANA** winked back.

I noted this as a definite SIGN of potential mischief and decided to keep my eye on both of them.

The TEA TENT was absolutely packed as apparently I am the only person in the whole W I D E world who has had it up to the armpits with baking and bunting. If I am absolutely honest, it did feel a bit exciting and the cakes did look very yummy. But NOT the bunting – that was just TRIANGLES.

Mrs Farquar-Haha and Georgina *barged* to the front of the tent and Mrs Farquar-Haha held her MEGAPHONE up for what I really hoped was the very LAST time that day. She SHRIEKED that although

everyone who had taken part in ANY competition today was a winner **of sorts** the ACTUAL **winner** was **actually** Georgina, and because she was such a **MASSIVE** winner Georgina was going to help her **judge** the BAKE-A-RAMA. I was surprised about that as I had sort of imagined Georgina would be **winning** this too, but Wilf explained to me that the BAKE-A-RAMA was just for the **grown-ups**. They only let children do a cupcake competition and **guess** who WON that? Yes, you are correct.

Anyway, all the CARDS that told you who had baked each cake had been folded over so NO ONE knew who had baked what – just like on the telly. That made it a bit more exciting, but only a BIT. Mrs Farquar-Haha and Georgina went along the row of cakes tasting

them ALL, and Georgina got to use her yoghurt-advert smile again while she ate lots and LOTS of delicious cakes. We all watched super closely as they tried Dad's coffee-and-walnut cake and they didn't spit it STRAIGHT out, so they obviously liked it more than me and I took that as a good sign.

Mrs Farquar-Haha and Georgina were taking so LONG to eat all the cakes that my tummy started to really rumble. The next cake looked especially pretty, with little red bits on the TOP and lovely oOozy red jam in the MIDDLE and my tummy started to feel quite cross that even though there was a tonne of cake about it wasn't getting ANY of it.

Then all of a sudden my tummy shut up because it was VERY distracted by the person next to me who was ACTUALLY shaking, and when I turned I saw that the person WAS in actual fact **BAD NANA** and she was clearly trying to keep a laugh IN, and we all know that when you keep a laugh IN it *shakes* out of your shoulders anyway.

My MISCHIEF ALERT went up to **12** and it has NEVER, ever gone to **12** before. I felt quite STRONGLY that *something* was about to happen . . .

169

Georgina and Mrs Farquar-Haha tasted a bit of the lovely cake with the pretty little red bits on TOP and the oOOzy red jam in the MIDDLE and they both looked *very* pleased. Then they tasted a bigger bit and did the yoghurt-advert smile at each other.

Then all of a SUDDEN their smiles disappeared completely and their eyes went HUGE and their lips went TINY and their cheeks went BRIGHT RED and a tiny bit of BAD NANA'S laugh *escaped* out of her mouth and I wondered what on earth would happen NEXT.

Once Mrs Farquar-Haha and Georgina had gulped the cake down, their mouths opened WIDER than their eyes and they seemed to be saying, "Oooogha₀aaahhhh ...Oooogha₀aaahhhh..." over and over.

Everyone looked around the tent as if that would suddenly help them understand what Georgina and Mrs Farquar-Haha were saying. Everyone except BAD NANA, who I suspected UNDERSTOOD much more about this than anyone else.

Cynth magically appeared with TWO glasses of WATER and, judging by the way Georgina and Mrs Farquar-Haha *snatched* them out of her hands and DOWNED them *SUPER FAST*, "Ooooghaₐₐaahhhh", actually does mean "water".

Mrs Farquar-Haha and Georgina went back to their normal colour again and

seemed okay, and you could tell that everyone in the whole tent was a bit RELIEVED. But then suddenly everyone was completely UNRELIEVED as Georgina and Mrs Farquar-Haha's faces went BRIGHT red all over again and they *RAN* out of the tent with actual smoke coming out of their ears. Maybe.

Dad walked over to the **pretty cake** they had been trying and, like one of the American **cops** he likes on the telly, he dabbed his finger into the **oozy** red jam and *LICKED* it. Then he tasted one of the pretty **red** bits from the TOP and in his

best American accent, which was actually quite good, he said, "*Chilli jam AND chilli flakes*" and the WHOLE tent gasped. I could tell he was really quite enjoying being a **cake detective** when he picked up the card and read, "*BAKED by . . .*

This cake was baked by...

Bad Nana

...BAD NANA!"

And everyone gasped AGAIN.
And then, *QUICK* as a *FLASH*, BAD NANA
gave everyone the BIG eyes and wobbly
old-lady smile and said that she knew
her traditional CHILLI CAKE wasn't to
everyone's taste, but it was an old
family recipe and it was a bit unusual, but
she had tried her very best and SORRY.

Amazingly, EVERYONE seemed to ACCEPT this, which just goes to show what you can GET AWAY with when you are really, really, really old and very good at wobbly smiles. Personally, I CAN'T WAIT.

Well, after ALL THAT the tannoy crickled and crackled and the announcer man who makes the announcements ANNOUNCED THAT . . .

There will be some

BAAAAAKE-AA

on account of the

NEW JUDGES for the RAAAAMMMAAAAAA OLD JUDGES only being able to taste HOT!

It sounded like he did a LITTLE laugh after he said that, but Dad said it was a cough. (It wasn't.)

Mr Cuthbert and Penny Heard's mum stepped in as the new JUDGES even though Marcy and Wilf and I offered. Then the best thing happened and Dad's coffee-and-walnut cake won the whole BAKE-A-RAMA, which just goes to show that some people think disgusting-tasting cakes are ACTUALLY really delicious.

And it really made such a nice CHANGE for someone **other** than Georgina to WIN, and although I was *quite* surprised I was mainly very pleased for Dad. He went all pink, but in a HAPPY way, not in a GOT-THE-PIP way. Even **BAD NANA** looked pleased and this made Dad go *even* pinker. Mum probably would have been pleased too, but she was still on the TOMBOLA stall.

After Dad was awarded his rosette for BAKE-A-RAMA, Mr Cuthbert was given the MEGAPHONE and said that despite a few hiccups here and there it really had been a VERY nice town fair day, and could anyone who entered any competition at all please GO into the SQUARE ring so everyone could give them a jolly BIG round of applause.

Wilf and Marcy and Jack and I and *even* Dad raced into the RING and

everyone was there, except Georgina, Mrs Farquar-Haha and Peanut. Marcy said she would tell Peanut all about it later and I'm NOT sure Georgina or Mrs Farquar-Haha would have been too keen on it anyway. But it really was VERY lovely to be there laughing and clapping with everyone and town fair day felt FAIR again. Mum even made it over for a clap as the TOMBOLA stall had finally run out of "prizes".

After all the competitions and shows and jolly BIG rounds of applause, there was only a LITTLE bit of town fair day left. **BAD NANA**, Cynth and Jack had a nice sit-down with a great BIG slice of Dad's disgusting coffee-and-walnut cake.

Mum and Dad did tidying up, which they really seem to LOVE, as they do it quite a LOT, and Marcy and Wilf and me had a lovely relaxing bounce on the bouncy castle.

And as we bouncED UP and DOWN
I realised a few things . . .

1. People really, really, really like TOMBOLAS, even if all they WIN are tins of soup and boring squash and stinky talc.

2. The SHOW really must go on.

3. COMPETITIONS are great, but only ONE person can win and *even* then they can win for something as REVOLTING as coffee-and-walnut cake, so being a winner is really just about making the cake that that exact judge thinks is nice.

4. HAMSTERS don't get out enough.

5. That *even* though BAD NANA is sometimes a bit naughty she is ALSO kind, cuddly, brave and fun . . . and I wouldn't SWAP her for anything.

6. Well, *maybe* a GIRAFFE, but **honestly** nothing else.

LOOK OUT for MORE BAD Nana mischief...